The Yellow Star

0 0 APR 2014

The Legend of

King Christian X

of Denmark

To Queen Margrethe II of Denmark

—H.S.

To the families and individuals of Decatur,

Georgia, who embraced my family

and hundreds of Cuban refugees

Special Thanks. To my daughters: Katie, who daily teaches me compassion by example; Erin, who tames children, animals, and her mother with her gentle spirit; and Lauren, whose wit and wisdom can make me laugh and cry. To the Safrans: Carden, whose beauty of mind and spirit can take my breath away; Claire, little hunnybunny; and Eric, true poet, honest friend, and my dear love.

Acknowledgments. The Royal Danish Embassy, Washington, D.C.; Carla Singer, Bremen Jewish Heritage Museum; Dr. Carol Harless; Steve Sanfield; Margaret Quinlin; Ryan Korn; Alex Panzer.

—C.A.D.

First published in the UK in 2002 by
Cat's Whiskers
96 Leonard Street
London EC2A 4XD

ISBN 1 903012 50 3 (hbk)
ISBN 1 903012 57 0 (pbk)

Text © 2000 by Carmen Agra Deedy
Illustrations © 2000 by Henri Sørensen
Originally published in the United States in 2000 by Peachtree Publishers, Atlanta, Georgia.
Book design by Loraine M. Balcsik

A CIP catalogue record for this book is available from the British Library

Printed in Singapore

The Yellow Star

The Legend of
King Christian X
of Denmark

Carmen Agra Deedy

Illustrated by
Henri Sørensen

CAT'S Whiskers
THE WATTS PUBLISHING GROUP LTD

Early in the year 1940,
in the country of Denmark,
there were only Danes.

Tall Danes.

Stout Danes.

Old Danes.

Silly Danes.

Cranky Danes.

...And even some Great Danes.

But no matter how different from each other they seemed, the Danes had one thing in common: all were loyal subjects of their beloved King Christian.

Every morning, their king rode alone and unarmed along the streets of Denmark's capital, Copenhagen.

"Who's that?" a curious visitor once asked.

"Why, that's our King Christian!" his Danish host responded.

"Without a bodyguard?" asked the astonished guest.

"My friend," came the proud reply, "a king so loved needs no bodyguard. We Danes would all stand together in defence of our king."

Little did the Danes know how much they would need their wise king in the dark days to come.

Like a fierce storm, war was spreading across Europe, and even good King Christian was powerless to stop it.

Soon Nazi soldiers gathered like dark clouds at the Danish border. Their arrival in Copenhagen brought food shortages, curfews, and a new flag, which was hung at the palace.

The flag stood for war and fear and hatred.

The Danes watched and waited to see what their king would do.

King Christian sent a Danish soldier to remove the flag.

Upon discovering it missing, a Nazi officer demanded to see the king and asked, "Who took down the flag?"

"I sent a soldier to remove it," replied the king.

"Oh, you did, did you? Well, tomorrow another will fly in its place," the officer boasted.

"Then tomorrow I will send another soldier to remove it," countered the king.

"And I will have that man shot," threatened the Nazi.

Leaning forward, King Christian said evenly, "Then be prepared to shoot the king — for I will be that soldier."

The Nazi flag did not fly from the palace again.

The missing flag became a powerful symbol of resistance, and King Christian's subjects found reasons to pass the palace gates to see where it had once hung.

Yet it was only a small victory; the king and his people's greatest test was still to come.

The terrible news arrived quietly, with leaflets that fluttered down on the city of Copenhagen:

Effective Immediately!

All Jews must sew onto their clothing a YELLOW STAR which must be visible AT ALL TIMES!

The people of Denmark were frightened. They had heard terrible stories. In some places, once Jews wore the yellow star, they were taken away and not heard from again.

As before, the people looked to their king.

This time their king was as frightened as his people.

Without the yellow star to point them out, the Jews looked like any other Danes. Gentiles and Jews were all Danish subjects who worshipped God in different ways.

If King Christian called on the tiny Danish army to fight, Danes would die. If he did nothing, Danes would die.

Perhaps it was this riddle of the yellow star that drew King Christian to his balcony that night. The sky was filled with the light of many stars.

"If you wished to hide a star," wondered the king to himself, "where would you place it?" His eyes searched the heavens.

"Of course!" he thought. The answer was so simple. "You would hide it among its sisters."

The king summoned his tailor.

The tailor arrived and listened to the king's surprising request.

"We only have an hour before I ride at dawn," the king said urgently. "Can you complete this task in time?"

"Yes, your Highness. I'll begin immediately." The tailor bowed respectfully.

"And you do understand what this means?" the king insisted.

"I do, Your Highness, as will all your subjects," he answered with pride.

"I trust they will," whispered the king, placing as much faith in his Danish subjects as they had in him.

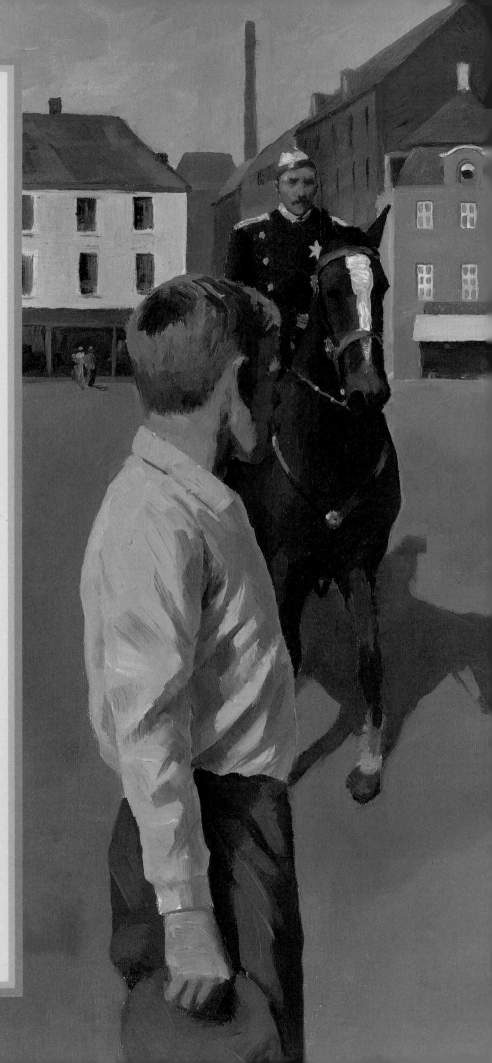

The following morning the King of Denmark, with courage and defiance, rode alone through Copenhagen. He was dressed in his finest clothing.

As they watched him pass, the subjects of King Christian understood what they should do.

And, once again, in the country of Denmark, there were only Danes.

Author's Note

*Legend: a traditional story sometimes popularly
regarded as historical but unauthenticated; a myth.*
—THE CONCISE OXFORD DICTIONARY, 8TH EDITION

The story of THE YELLOW STAR is a legend. It may be disappointing to
the reader as it first was to this author to learn there is no proof that
the story ever happened. I learned of it as a scrap of a tale told to me
by a stranger. Its imagery was so compelling, and its humanity so
palpable, that I wanted to know more. Over the years, despite
collecting various oral versions of the story, researching documents
and works of fiction (most notably Lois Lowry's moving novel, NUMBER
THE STARS), I found only *unauthenticated* references to King Christian's
legendary defiance.

And I learned of many facts that in their own right were as powerful
as the legend itself. I learned that

- The beloved King of Denmark did indeed ride unescorted and
  unprotected through the streets of Copenhagen.

- Stories about the king's support of Danish Jews began to
  circulate throughout Europe as early as 1943, including his
  threat to wear the yellow star in solidarity with the Jews.

- No Jews within Denmark were forced to wear the yellow star.

- Among the Nazi-occupied countries, only Denmark rescued the overwhelming majority of its Jews.

- Over 7,000 Danish Jews were smuggled to Sweden in fishing boats, 12 to 14 at a time, by a group of Danes called the "Helsingor Sewing Club".

- Of the almost 500 Danish Jews deported to Theresienstadt concentration camp, all but 51 survived, in large part owing to the Danish government's intercession on their behalf.

Yet the legend only grows stronger. Why? Perhaps because we need it. The allegory of the yellow star used by the Nazis to divide and shame became in this legend a symbol of unity and hope. It is a story that should be told.

What if it *had* happened? What if every Dane, from shoemaker to priest, had worn the yellow Star of David?

And what if we could follow that example today against violations of human rights? What if the good and strong people of the world stood shoulder to shoulder, crowding the streets and filling the squares, saying, "You cannot do this injustice to our sisters and brothers, or you must do it to us as well."

What if?

—C. A. D.
2000